"We are not only the age we are
but all the ages we have ever been."
-Fred Rogers

the Bora Boys and the Last Big Door

written by
Michael J. Feeney

illustrated by
John Devaney

the Bora Boys and the Last Big Door

This is the first of a series of "Bora Boys" books.
To order books or to obtain permission to reproduce selections from this book contact us at:
www.theboraboys.com -on the web, info@theboraboys.com -email, or write us at
M.J. Feeney & Sons, 38 Orange Street, Nantucket, MA 02554.

Written by Michael J. Feeney
Artwork by John Devaney
Layout & design by Bruce Marshall-Jones
Production by Color Graphics, Nantucket Island

Printed in China

Library of Congress Control Number 2003098703

ISBN: 0-9746266-0-0

A portion of the proceeds of the sale of this book will be donated to **The Sharing Foundation**,
to benefit Cambodia's children. www.sharingfoundation.org

Special Thanks to

Rebekah Mannix
Annye Camara
Bruce Marshall-Jones
Bob Barsanti
Mary Miles

M. J. FEENEY & SONS
NANTUCKET

Dedicated to my wife Bernadette,
without whose encourgement, faith and love
none of this could have happened.

Jack Bora and his little brother, Mickey, live on a little island called Nantucket in a very big and very old house called The Four Chimneys.

Jack and Mickey do everything together: play, eat, take baths, and sleep. What they love most is to have adventures.

One day at naptime, Jack and Mickey could not fall asleep. Jack decided that exploring the attic would be more exciting than lying awake in bed. "ObaKabee!" Mickey agreed clapping his tiny hands. The boys had never been to the attic because Mom and Dad said it was too high up for them. Together, they climbed down from their bed, quietly tiptoed out of the bedroom and up the hall to the forbidden stairs that led to the Last Big Door. Up and up they climbed to the top. Jack reached for the shimmering crystal doorknob but could not turn it with just the tips of his fingers. "I...can't...reach...enough," he said.

"OhbaNobo", Mickey said, looking up at his brother.

Just when they were about to give up, the door, all by itself, slowly opened with an eerie, creaking moan.

"It's so dark inside, Mickey," said Jack.
"I see a light over there. Follow me!"

The two brave boys crept through the dark
toward the mysterious beacon that seemed to be
calling to them. The darkness surrounding them
was full of strange things that made them a little
scared. But only a little.

Finally, they made it to the light. And what
a sight it was!

Looming before them was a ship's ladder
that looked as though it went all the way to the sky!

Jack and Mickey looked up and up and were beginning to wonder if they should go back to their bedroom, when they heard a voice calling to them from way up the mysterious ladder.

"Hellooo, Mateys! I've been expecting you!"

Jack and Mickey grabbed for each other in fright and closed their eyes!

"Are you just gonna sit there blubbering like a couple o' lubbers, or are you gonna come on up here and have the adventure you was lookin' for?" said the voice.

Even though they were scared, Jack could tell that the voice was friendly, so he gathered up his courage and started to climb the ladder. Mickey didn't want to be left alone, so he followed. "Don't look down, Mickey," said Jack.

When Jack finally got to the top, he climbed into a bright, sunny room and quickly helped his little brother up. When they were both safely in, they ran to the windows and were amazed.

"Wow! Look, Mickey," Jack said. "You can see everything up here!"

"You can't see everything yet. That takes some time," said a voice.

Jack and Mickey spun around and came face to face with what appeared to be...a ghost! The two boys stood frozen, unable to move. It was a big ghost with a friendly, round face sporting a bushy grey beard. He was dressed in clothes from days gone by, like the ones Jack had seen in the Whaling Museum. He had a big jolly belly and stood on one full leg. The other was a white ivory peg from the knee down. And they could see right through him! It was as though he was made of fog.

"Hello, Mateys," said the ghost. "My name is Captain Whalebone N. Tucket... at your service."

The ghost bowed so low in front of them that his chin rested on the floorboards as he continued to examine his two new friends with one opened eye. He looked so funny bowing there that Jack and Mickey actually started to laugh.

"Now then, that's more like my boys!" said the ghost. "Please, just call me Whalebone." Then he stuck out his big, foggy hand for them to shake, and they did.

"What's your name, little fella?" said Whalebone to Mickey.

"Vacuum," said Mickey. Jack laughed and told Whalebone that vacuum was just Mickey's favorite word, and it meant that Mickey liked him.

"Well, I like you, too, Mickey my boy! And you, big fella – what might your name be?" asked Whalebone.

"My name is Jack Bora," said Jack proudly.

"Well, Jack Bora, it's a pleasure to meet such a handsome young shipmate. Where do you hail from – Cochin China?"

"Huh?" said Jack.

"I said, where ya from, Matey?"

"Oh," said Jack. "Well, I live right here with my family."

"Jackabobadid," said little Mickey with a grin.

"What's that?", asked Whalebone.

"Jackabobadid an mefummommatumtum," said Mickey, absolutely pleased with himself.

"Well, little Mickey, I've heard every language there is to hear, but this one's got me stumped! Now let's see," said Whalebone, stroking his long beard and deep in thought. "Hmmm. Jackabobadid an mefummommatumtum...hummm. Hold on... I've got it!" said the Captain triumphantly. "You're sayin' Jack's adopted...and me from Momma's tummy! Isn't that what you're sayin', Mickey?"

"Yay!" said Mickey clapping his hands.

"That's it!" said Jack. "I'm from Adopted!"

"Well, Jack Bora, I've been everywhere in the world a hundred times, and I can tell where anyone's from, and you look to me to be a young fella from Kampuchea."

"Where?" asked Jack.

"Kampuchea...you know, Cambodia, I think they call it nowadays", said Whalebone.

"Cam-bo-di-a...Cambodia! I hear my Mom and Dad say that word a lot!" said Jack.

"What do you say we go on a trip, boys... a trip to Kampuchea... a trip to Cambodia. Do you want some adventure?"

"VACUUM!" said Mickey. "But what about Mom and Dad?" Jack wondered.

"Now you listen here, Jack Bora!" Whalebone said, smiling. "I'm a ghost, and I'm magic. I'll have you back here before your naptime is over. What do you say?"

"OK, Whalebone. Let's Go!" said Jack.

"All right, boys. Just climb up here and sit on old Whalebone's knee and look out yonder at old Nantucket Harbor, and I'll tell you a story about far away and long ago."

Jack and Mickey climbed onto Whalebone's lap. It was so comfortable and warm and smelled like the sea. As they snuggled together and looked out the window at the Harbor, Whalebone began to speak.

"Far away...and long ago..." The room filled with a warm fog and the boys fell fast asleep.

Jack awoke to the crowing of a rooster. Mickey lay next to him, still sleeping. Jack had a funny feeling that he wasn't home in Nantucket any more. But he wasn't scared. He felt very comfortable and familiar with where he was. The house was open and airy. There were no glass windows. A warm breeze that smelled like flowers traveled freely through the room. He and Mickey had been sleeping on straw mats.

Jack walked to the door and looked outside. He felt as if he was living a dream he sometimes had. There was field after field of long grasses where people were working slowly and steadily. Tall palm trees lined the horizon. Children played along a dirt road. The house he was in was built on poles high off the ground. Nearby, there was a cow tied to a fence, lazily chewing on the little plants around her feet.

Mickey laughed out loud in his sleep and turned over on the mat, reaching for his brother.

"I thought you'd never wake up!" said a voice. Jack spun around with a start, but broke into a big smile at the sight of old Whalebone in an sarong, preparing some food over a small fire in the corner.

"Whalebone!" said Jack, "Where are we? What happened? How did we get here? I can't see through you any more!"

"Whoa! Slow down there, young fella," said Whalebone. "All your questions'll be answered soon enough. Now you'd better wake up that little brother of yours. We have a lot to do today!"

"OK, Whalebone," said Jack. "Mickey, wake up!" he said, gently shaking his little brother.

Mickey woke up laughing, stood up, and started dancing on the sleeping mat for no particular reason. Jack started dancing, too. Both of the boys were dancing, spinning, jumping up and down, and laughing.

"Ahoy there, Mateys. Grub is up," said Whalebone. The boys ran over to the Captain and sat with him on the floor. He gave them noodle soup and steamed dumplings. "Boys, in case you haven't already figured it out, we're in Cambodia and this is a Cambodian breakfast!"

"It's good!" said Jack as he hungrily ate up the delicious food.

"Hot! Hot!" said Mickey as he pointed to the steam rising from his noodle soup.

When they had finished their meal, Jack and Mickey followed Whalebone down the wooden stairs to the ground below.

"Whalebone, why can't we see through you any more?" Jack asked as he and Mickey watched him hitch the cow up to a wooden cart.

"Well, because I brought you back to my living time," he said. "You see, we're in Cambodia, but we're also in the year 1860. I can only take you on adventures if they occur during the time when I was alive. Those are the rules of Ghost Transportation. I didn't make 'em, but I gotta follow 'em."

"I see," said Jack, with a puzzled look on his face.

"Mooo!" said Mickey, who was pulling the cow's tail.

"Whalebone, are we going to ride in that cart with the cow pulling us?" asked Jack excitedly.

"We sure are, boys!" Whalebone gently lifted Jack and Mickey into the cart, where they sat toward the back; and the Captain sat on a seat up front behind the cow. He took the reins in his big hands, looked back over his shoulder at Mickey and Jack, and said, "Hold on, boys — we're goin' for a ride to Prey Sar to see the annual oxcart races!"

"Yay!" said Mickey and Jack.

As the three adventurers wheeled happily along through forests and rice paddies, Whalebone explained to the boys that for many centuries, at the end of the harvest season, farmers would thank their cows for all their hard work by bathing them and giving them gifts of food. The farmers would sometimes even perfume the cows with aromatic oils and powders. By the time the Khmer New Year came around (in the month we call April), the strongest and most beautiful cows were chosen to participate in the ancient oxcart races.

The quiet countryside changed as they approached Prey Sar. There were many houses decorated with colorful flags in celebration of the New Year. The red dirt road was lined with tall banners of green, yellow, and white. There were many people laughing and standing around roadside stands where food was sold. The air was full of delicious smells. Whalebone drove the cart to a well in the busy town square. He tied the cow up to a post and drew a wooden bucket of water from which she drank gratefully.

"Whalebone, help us down!" said Jack, who was eager to join in the festivities going on all around him. The Captain lifted the boys out of the cart and put them down on the ground.

"Now boys, hear this — stay close to old Whalebone so you don't get lost."

Jack and Mickey had never seen anything so exciting or beautiful. There were jugglers and dancers and people playing music with homemade instruments. Whalebone brought the boys to a sweet-smelling stand where he bought some snacks.

"You want some candy, boys?"

"Yeah!" said Jack and Mickey. They each got a snack that looked like caramel popcorn wrapped up in a green leaf. They all sat down by the side of the road and ate up their warm, crunchy snacks. As they watched, three young girls with golden robes danced a slow, graceful, Cambodian dance called a lamthon while their father played a kind of violin with only one string. When they were all finished, Mickey tugged on Whalebone's sarong and said, "Mo...mo...mo eat!"

"What's that, Mickey? You want some more crickets?" said Whalebone.

"Huh?" said Jack. "Did you say crickets?"

"Sure!" said Whalebone. "That tasty snack was honey-roasted crickets wrapped up in lotus leaves. Want some more?"

"Oh, no thanks," said Jack, as he put his hand on his tummy. Mickey said, "Mo...mo keekit...mo keekit!"

Just then, two men beating a large brass gong came striding up the red dirt road. Everyone followed them to a big green field. Whalebone sat Mickey up on his shoulder, took Jack's hand, and followed the happy crowd. "The oxcart races are beginning!" he announced to Mickey and Jack.

"Whalebone, I can't see!" said Jack. Whalebone lifted him up with one strong hand and sat him on a big tree branch, where Jack happily called out, "Now I can see everything!"

Up at the head of the field, there were many teams of powerful oxen, or cows, whose horns and heads were brightly decorated in silk and feathers. Their bridles were festooned with tiny bells that chimed when the cows moved their necks. The praeks, or cart frames, were hung with colorful little flags and feathers. The drivers were strong, serious-looking men with red and blue scarves wrapped around the top of their heads like turbans. They looked as though they really wanted to win the race that was about to begin.

While the drivers struggled to hold the racing cows still, all the people fell silent as a bhikkhu, or Buddhist monk, performed a blessing. When he finished, he smiled, held up his arms, and shouted, "Sur sdey chnam thmey!" Happy new year! and the crowd broke into a loud and happy cheer.

"Yay!" said Jack.

"Mo! Mo keekit!" said Mickey as he pulled on Whalebone's ear from his shoulder perch.

Four carts, four drivers, and four cows all lined up at the head of the field. Men on the ground held the teams in place. A loud gong pierced the air. Everyone could feel the excitement! The men on the ground ran away and the cows bellowed and snorted as their powerful bodies bolted into motion. The drivers took off in the speeding praeks, whipping the reins and screaming, "YEEEAAHHH!"

Whalebone, Jack, and Mickey cheered as the racers stormed toward them. Mickey grabbed onto Whalebone's hair and Jack clung to the tree. As the spectacle came nearer and nearer, the cows seemed to get bigger and bigger. As the teams rounded the bend where the three adventurers were perched, dirt, stones, and grass flew off the charging hooves and speeding wheels into the crowd. In a choking cloud of dust, the thundering teams rounded the bend.

The roaring crowd, the screaming drivers, the pounding hooves, and the swirling whirlwind of red dust was just plain too much for Mickey. The kindly Whalebone knew Mickey was scared and snatched him and Jack away from the wild crowd to a quiet, grassy place under a banyon tree.

After a long silence, Whalebone finally spoke up: "How was that for an adventure?"

Jack and Mickey were speechless. Eventually, Mickey looked up at Whalebone's friendly face and said, "Mo keekit...mo keekit..." Whalebone and Jack broke into a long and hearty belly laugh!

"Mo keekit...mo keekit...mo keekit," they sang together as they walked back to their own cow and praek.

As they happily wheeled their way home through the lush green Cambodian countryside,
Whalebone made up songs to sing, such as "Yo Ho Ho and a Bottle of Keekits!"

When they got back to the quiet little house on stilts, Whalebone unhitched their faithful old cow and tied her up to the fence, where she started munching on the little plants again.

As the silvery new moon rose in the sky, Whalebone cooked a Cambodian supper of rice and fish, which they all ate up as they laughed and talked about the adventure they had had today. Afterward, the boys grew very sleepy. Mickey and Jack missed their parents, who usually tucked them in. Mickey cried, "Where Momma? Where Momma?"

Whalebone instructed the boys to climb up onto his lap, which they did. Jack yawned, and with sleepy eyes he asked, "Whalebone, can we ever come back to Cambodia?"

"Why, sure we can, Matey. There's a whole big, beautiful world I want you to see. Now hush...and I'll tell you a story of long ago and far away..."

A warm fog filled the room and the boys fell fast asleep.

"Jack! Mickey! It's time to wake up, my two little boys," said a voice. Jack and Mickey sat up and rubbed their eyes. They were astonished to find that they were back in their own bed!

"Hi, Mommy! I'm from Kampuchea — that means Cambodia!" Jack said.

"Why, that's...that's right, honey," his mother said, somewhat taken aback as Jack jumped out of bed and headed for the dressing room. "Let's go and get dressed, Mickey," she said, picking little Mickey up and following Jack.

As they were walking up the hallway, Mickey looked over his Momma's shoulder and up the staircase to the Last Big Door. He felt certain he saw Whalebone's smiling face in the crystal doorknob, beckoning him.

Mickey smiled as a voice only he could hear called to him, saying, "Remember, Mickey, whenever you want adventure and tales of yore, Old Whalebone'll be waitin' behind the Last Big Door."